This
**PJ BOOK**
belongs to

PJ Library®

JEWISH BEDTIME STORIES and SONGS

# Netta and Her Plant

Then something wonderful happened, my family grew!
This story is for my grandchildren, and their friends.
To Neta, Avital, and especially for Noam, the one who really
has a Tu B'Shevat birthday. —E.G.

To Sergio, Greta, and Leonardo with love —N.U.

KAR-BEN PUBLISHING
A division of Lerner Publishing Group, Inc.
241 First Avenue North
Minneapolis, MN 55401 U.S.A.
1-800-4-KARBEN

Website address: www.karben.com

Library of Congress Cataloging-in-Publication Data

Gellman, Ellie B.
    Netta and her plant / by Ellie B. Gellman ; illustrated by Natascia Ugliano.
        pages   cm.
    Summary: When Netta is very small, her preschool teacher gives her a plant for Tu B'Shevat
and as the years pass, both Netta and her plant grow and change.
      ISBN 978–1–4677–0422–9 (lib. bdg. : alk. paper)
      ISBN 978–1–4677–2435–7 (eBook)
      [1. Growth—Fiction. 2. Plants—Fiction. 3. Tu bi-Shevat—Fiction. 4. Jews—Fiction.]
    I. Ugliano, Natascia illustrator. II. Title.
    PZ7.G2835Net 2014
    [E]—dc23                                                    2013002192

Manufactured in China
1 – PN – 10/25/13

011425K1

# Netta and Her Plant

by Ellie B. Gellman

illustrated by Natascia Ugliano

KAR-BEN
PUBLISHING

"It's Tu B'Shevat today," the teacher explained. "Your name, Netta, means 'plant,' and now is the time to plant. We can plant this seedling together."

Netta brought her plant home. Her Ima put it on the small table in the living room. "We can take care of it together."

Netta liked to play in the living room. She put together puzzles and built a tower with her blocks. Netta tried to make the tower as tall as her plant.

"Plants like to hear music," said Ima, so Netta sang her favorite songs while she played.

The plant grew. Netta grew.

It was Tu B'Shevat again.
Ima said to Netta," You are too big for your
little bed. It's time to buy you a bigger one."

Ima and Abba took Netta to the furniture store.
They bought a big bed. Netta picked out a quilt
covered with trees and plants and flowers.

When they got home, Netta looked at her plant.
"You are too big for that pot," she said. "You
need a bigger pot." So Ima and Abba took
Netta to the garden shop to buy a bigger pot.

They helped her put the plant in the new pot and add new dirt. Netta took her crayons and drew trees and plants and flowers on a piece of paper and wrapped it around the new pot.

The plant grew. Netta grew.

On her birthday, Netta came home from school
wearing a crown of flowers. She carefully lifted
it off her head and put it around her plant.
"Now you can celebrate, too," Netta said.

The plant grew. Netta grew.

Then something surprising happened. Her Ima grew, too! Just after school ended for the summer, Netta had a little sister. Her name was Avital. Abba explained that "tal" is the word for dew. He told her dew helps to water plants so that they grow.

Ima was very busy taking care of Avital, but Netta didn't mind. She was very busy taking care of her plant. Savta came over and helped Netta water the plant by herself without spilling.

Then she helped Savta give Avital a drink of water. And she didn't spill any.

The plant grew. Netta grew.

One day Ima and Abba told Netta that they were moving to a new, bigger house. It was too crowded in their apartment.

Netta wasn't sure she wanted to move. "It will be OK," Ima said. "In the new house you will have your own room."

Netta told her plant that soon they would be moving. "You don't have to be afraid. It will be OK, and in the new house you will have your own room."

On moving day, Netta hurried to help Ima put her
special quilt on the bed in her new bedroom.

Then she put the plant on the porch. "You will be the first one to see the sun every morning," she said.

The plant grew. Netta grew.

The summer was over. It was time for kindergarten. Netta wasn't sure she wanted to go to a new school. Abba told her that she was big enough and that she would make new friends.

Netta went out to the porch to talk to her plant. Its leaves leaned past the edge of the pot, and the stem reached above the railing. "You've grown so much, it's time for you to go live by yourself," Netta said. "Tomorrow before I start my new school, Abba will help me plant you in a garden, where you can make new friends."

Netta and Abba put the plant in a big basket. They walked across two streets and turned a corner. Behind Netta's new school was a park. They chose a sunny spot, and planted Netta's plant beside a tall tree.

The plant grew. Netta grew.

On the first day of kindergarten, Netta took
a friend to meet her plant.

"This is Ilana, my new friend," she said to the plant. " 'Ilana' means 'tree.' Look at all the trees that grow in this park! They will be your friends. When it is Tu B'Shevat again the trees will have a birthday and so will you! Ilana and I will come to visit you, with all of our new friends, and we will have a party."

# And that is what they did.

## Glossary of Hebrew Words

Abba — Father
Ima — Mother
Morah — Teacher
Savta — Grandmother

## About Tu B'Shevat

Tu B'Shevat, the 15th day of the month of Shevat, is the Jewish New Year for trees. While it is winter in much of the world, in Israel the almond trees are beginning to bloom, announcing the start of spring. Children gather with shovels to plant new saplings. In places where it is too cold to plant, families celebrate with fruit-tasting parties, often sampling fruits grown in Israel such as almonds, oranges, figs, dates, olives, and carob.

### About the Author

Ellie Gellman grew up in Minneapolis, Minnesota, where she first began telling stories to the children in her synagogue. She has taught in Jewish schools in the United States, Canada, and Israel. Her previous books include *Jeremy's Dreidel*, and *Tamar's Sukkah.* She lives in Jerusalem and has four children and two grandchildren.

### About the Illustrator

Natascia Ugliano received her diploma at the Fine Arts Academy of Brera, in Milan, Italy. She has illustrated many children's books including *Abraham's Search for God, Sarah Laughs,* and *Benjamin and the Silver Goblet.* She lives in Milan.